Enid Bl

Mr Pink-Whistle's Party

Text illustrations by Kevin Kimber
Cover illustration by Val Biro

AWARD PUBLICATIONS LIMITED

Enid Blyton's Happy Days!

Snowball the Pony

Bimbo and Topsy

Run-About's Holiday

The Adventures of Binkle and Flip

Binkle and Flip Misbehave

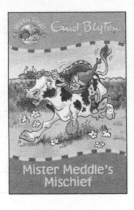
Mister Meddle's Mischief

Mister Meddle's Muddles

Merry Mister Meddle

You're a Nuisance Mister Meddle

Collect all the titles in the series!

The Adventures of
Mr Pink-Whistle

Mr Pink-Whistle
Has Some Fun

Mr Pink-Whistle's
Party

Mr Pink-Whistle
Interferes

Hello
Mr Twiddle!

Mr Twiddle
in Trouble Again

Don't Be Silly,
Mr Twiddle!

Mr Twiddle
in Trouble Again

Shuffle
the Shoemaker

For further information on Enid Blyton please visit *www.blyton.com*

ISBN 978-1-84135-661-7

First published by George Newnes

First published by Award Publications Limited 2004
This edition first published 2010

Published by Award Publications Limited,
The Old Riding School, The Welbeck Estate,
Worksop, Nottinghamshire, S80 3LR

11 2

Printed in the United Kingdom

Contents

Chapter 1

Mr Pink-Whistle's Party

You remember Mr Pink-Whistle, don't you – the little man with pointed ears who goes about the world putting wrong things right? He's half a brownie, and can make himself invisible if he wants to.

Mr Pink-Whistle often passed a little house called Merry-Chimneys. He liked that name – and he liked the little girl who lived there.

She always seemed to be swinging on her garden gate when he passed. She smiled at him and waved cheerily. One day he stopped and spoke to her.

'What's your name? It ought to be Smiley, because you're always smiling!'

The little girl laughed. 'Well, my name is *almost* as good as that,' she said. 'It's Merry.'

'Ah – Merry by name and merry by nature,' said Mr Pink-Whistle. 'Very nice. But do tell me – why are you so often out here swinging on your gate?'

'Oh, don't you know?' said the little girl. 'It's because there's a *"Please Cross Here"* sign.'

Mr Pink-Whistle looked surprised. He had certainly seen the *"Please Cross Here"* sign, and had noticed the thick white lines painted across the road, just opposite the little girl's house. But what had that got to do with swinging on a gate?

'You look puzzled!' said Merry. 'I'll

explain. Well, my mother says everyone ought to do something to help other people, and if we can't see something we've got to look for it. Mother said I'd got something right at the front gate – helping people over the busy crossing. Cars are supposed to stop, but they don't always.'

'Show me what you do,' said Mr Pink-Whistle.

'Well, look – there's a Toddlers' Home three doors away,' said Merry. 'And I'm waiting for the nurses to come out with the children, so that I can help them across the road. They have to wheel prams with four or five babies in them, so they can't very well look after the children who are walking, too. Here they come. Now watch.'

Merry skipped down from the gate and went to meet two nurses and a crowd of tiny children walking hand-in-hand in twos.

They were chattering like sparrows. The nurses had an enormous pram each with children in them. What a weight to push along!

'Hello, Merry. There's Merry! Merry, take my hand!' called the tiny children. The nurses nodded and smiled at the little girl,

9

and went across the crossing with their prams. Merry carefully took every small child across herself, even holding up her hand to stop a car that was coming along.

When they had all gone over safely she skipped back to Mr Pink-Whistle. 'There you are,' she said. It's only a very little job, but it's a help, isn't it?'

'It certainly is,' said Mr Pink-Whistle. 'You did that well. Are you going in now you've done your job?'

'I've just got to wait for old Mr Lame and poor Mrs Limp,' said Merry. 'They come along about this time and somebody just has to help them across. They go so slowly, you see, and they are frightened of the cars. Here's Mr Lame.'

Pink-Whistle watched Merry guide the lame old fellow across the road. She chattered away to him, keeping a sharp eye out all the time for traffic. As soon as she got back to Pink-Whistle along came Mrs Limp. One of her legs was much shorter than the other, and she *really* couldn't hurry.

Merry took the limping woman safely across and carried her basket. Then she ran back again.

'Now I'm going in,' she said. 'I always know the time to come and swing on my gate and wait for all these people. Sometimes I come out just in case there might be somebody else afraid to cross – when I have a minute to spare. I suppose you wouldn't like me to help you across, would you?'

'I don't have to cross just here,' said Pink-Whistle. 'But thank you all the same. I'm glad to know you, Merry. There aren't many people like you in the world.'

The next time Mr Pink-Whistle passed by Merry's house, she waved to him again. 'Mr Pink-Whistle!' she called. 'Aren't I lucky! I'm going to a big party tomorrow, and I've got a new blue dress and blue shoes to match.'

'How lovely!' said Pink-Whistle. 'Well, you deserve a party, Merry.'

'There's going to be an enormous cake with candles,' said Merry. 'And a Punch and Judy Show – fancy that! And each child is to have two balloons and a present. Aren't I *lucky*!'

'I'll come by tomorrow morning at this time and you can show me your blue shoes,' said Mr Pink-Whistle. 'You get them out ready for me to see.'

But when he came the next day, there was no Merry swinging on the gate. He couldn't see her at all, not even at one of the windows. What could have happened?

'Perhaps she has gone shopping,' thought Pink-Whistle, and he waited a few minutes for her to come back. But she didn't. So Pink-Whistle walked up to the front door and rang the bell. A housekeeper answered the door and Pink-Whistle asked for Merry.

'She's out in the back garden,' said the

housekeeper. 'Would you like to go and find her?'

So out into the garden went Pink-Whistle and looked all round. There was a big lawn first, then an orchard, and then a kitchen garden. He couldn't see Merry anywhere. He walked down, puzzled.

No one was on the lawn. No one was in the orchard. Was anyone in the kitchen garden? No, there was nobody there, either.

There was a little garden shed nearby, and Mr Pink-Whistle thought he heard a noise coming from it – just a little noise. He went up and peeped in.

Yes. Merry was there – but what a different Merry! No smiles now, no merry laughter. She sat huddled up in a corner on an old sack, crying all by herself.

'What's the matter?' said Pink-Whistle, walking in and sitting down beside her.

'Oh, dear – you made me jump!' said Merry, wiping her eyes and giving him a very watery smile. 'Fancy you coming and finding me here!'

'Why aren't you out swinging on your gate as usual?' asked Pink-Whistle.

'I'm not allowed to for three whole weeks,'

said Merry dismally. 'You see, I had a little friend to tea yesterday – and this morning her mother came to tell my mother that she's got measles. So I'm not allowed to swing on the front gate, or talk to any other children for three weeks, in case I get it too, and give it to someone else.'

'That's very bad luck,' said Pink-Whistle. 'Very bad luck indeed. What about that party you were telling me of?'

'Well, of course, I can't possibly go to that,' said Merry, beginning to cry again. 'I'm sorry I'm so silly about it, but I just can't help feeling awfully disappointed. About my blue shoes and blue dress, you know – and not seeing the Punch and Judy Show. After all, I haven't been naughty or anything, have I? It isn't my fault.'

'It isn't – and you don't deserve such a disappointment,' said Pink-Whistle, comfortingly. 'But it just so happens that *I'm* giving a Punch and Judy party this afternoon, and *I'm* going to have an enormous cake with candles on, and there'll be balloons too – so you'll be able to come to that!'

Merry looked at him in astonishment. 'Are you *really* giving a party like that?' she said.

'But – I still won't be able to come, because I mustn't mix with other people.'

'Oh, that's all right,' said Pink-Whistle, cheerfully. 'My guests can't get measles, so you can mix with them all you like. Shall we have the party down here in the orchard?'

'*Could* we? Because I'm not allowed to go anywhere by bus or train,' said Merry, her eyes beginning to shine. 'But why can't your guests get measles? I thought anybody could get them.'

'Not *my* guests,' said Pink-Whistle, getting up. 'Well, put on your blue shoes and your blue dress this afternoon, and be here at three o'clock. Don't forget.'

He went off, leaving the little girl in such a state of excitement that she danced round every tree in the orchard. What a funny, wonderful little man Mr Pink-Whistle is!'

At three o'clock, dressed in her blue shoes and blue dress, with a blue ribbon in her hair, Merry ran down to the orchard. Good gracious me! What had happened to it!

Every tree was hung with streamers and shining ornaments. Great big toadstools had sprung up from the grass for tables and seats. Twelve had grown close together to make an extra big table for the guests to sit at.

The guests were coming from every direction. But they weren't children. Oh no – Mr Pink-Whistle had chosen his other kind of friends – the pixies and elves and brownies. There they came, trooping along, all dressed in their best, too!

Mr Pink-Whistle was welcoming them all, smiling even more broadly than usual. He saw Merry and went up to her. 'You look lovely in your blue shoes and blue dress,' he

said. 'I'm so glad you could come to my party. Now let me tell you who's here. This is Tiptoe – and this is Jinky – and this is Silky – and this is Jolly – and this is Heyho – dear me, I hope you'll remember all their names!'

Merry liked all the little people at once. She played games with them, ate the ice-creams that kept appearing on the little mushroom tables, and drank glasses of honey-lemonade. Lovely!

The tea was simply glorious. Merry counted twelve different kinds of most extraordinary sandwiches, and twelve different kinds of cakes. There were wobbly jellies and fruit salads with ice-cream on top. And oh, the cake, the cake that stood in the middle of the big table!

It shone and glittered with a hundred coloured candles, and it was decorated with silver and gold balls, pink, yellow and white icing, and all kinds of sugared flowers that could be eaten.

'See what's written on the top, Merry,' said Pink-Whistle. Merry looked and went red with pleasure.

'WELCOME TO MERRY!' was written in pink icing.

'Yes, it's *your* cake,' said Pink-Whistle. 'Made specially for you. Now – what about cutting it?'

After tea there was a Punch and Judy Show. It was much better than any show Merry had ever seen, and she laughed so much that she got a stitch.

Everyone had two balloons. 'They won't burst,' said Pink-Whistle. 'They've got just a touch of magic in them. They'll last for years.'

It was the loveliest party Merry had ever been to. At the end every guest had a present in a little shiny box. They all lined up and went to Pink-Whistle one by one.

'Thank you, Mr Pink-Whistle,' each little guest said. 'Thank you for having me to your lovely party. Goodbye!'

Merry said the same – and she gave the kind little man a sudden hug. 'You planned your party for *me*, I know you did!' she said. 'It's the nicest one I've ever been to. I love you, Mr Pink-Whistle. You go round the world putting things right – and that's what *I'm* going to do too!'

'You do it already – that's why I gave this party for you,' said Pink-Whistle. Well, goodbye, and I hope you'll like your present. I'll look out for you on the gate in three weeks' time!'

Merry opened her parcel when she got indoors. You will never guess what was inside! Very neatly folded, wrapped carefully in tissue paper, was – a pair of silvery wings! There was a little note tied to them.

'These can be fitted on your shoulders and used on every full-moon night. Please put away carefully when not in use.'

'What a present!' said Merry, softly, in the greatest delight. 'Wings! Wings of my own!' She shook them out gently, and looked at the calendar on the wall.

'Oh, dear – it won't be a full-moon night for ten days! How can I possibly wait?'

She'll have to wait, of course – but won't she be pleased to go flying in the garden when the moon is big and round and shiny! Dear old Pink-Whistle – he does know how to make people happy, doesn't he?

Chapter 2

Mr Pink-Whistle at Work Again

One day, when Mr Pink-Whistle was sitting eating an egg for his breakfast, his pointed ears heard something far away. Sooty, his cat, looked at him. She could hear something, too.

'It's somebody crying,' said Mr Pink-Whistle, getting up in a hurry. 'It sounds like a child. I haven't time to finish my toast, Sooty. I'll be back soon, I hope.'

Mr Pink-Whistle hurried to put on his hat, and then went down the garden path at top speed. He could still hear that crying.

He hopped on a bus, and went for some way, and then hopped off again. He stood and listened, his pointed ears moving like a dog's. Ah – the crying was somewhere over there – somewhere near that cottage.

Off he went, stepping softly, and soon he came to where a little girl was sitting, leaning against an old wall. She wasn't crying very loudly, as you might have thought because of Mr Pink-Whistle hearing her so far away, but quite softly.

'What's the matter?' asked Mr Pink-Whistle. The little girl looked up. She wasn't at all afraid to see Mr Pink-Whistle, his green eyes were so kind.

'Oh – did you hear me crying?' she said. 'I thought I was being very quiet.'

'Yes. I heard you,' said Mr Pink-Whistle, and he sat down beside her. 'Now – what's the matter? I'm Mr Pink-Whistle, and I try to put wrong things right. Maybe I can put something right for you?'

'Oh – are you really Mr Pink-Whistle?' said the little girl, in delight. 'I've read about you, and I always wanted to meet you. But I'm afraid you can't put things right for *me*.'

'You tell me, and I'll see,' said Pink-Whistle, and he took out a big bag of peppermints. 'Let's have one of these while we talk.'

'Well, it's like this,' said the little girl, taking a peppermint. 'I haven't got a father or mother, so my auntie looks after me. She's not very fond of me, really, because she thinks it's a nuisance to have me to see to. But she's all I've got. And now she's getting married and going out to Canada – so, of course, she doesn't want me any more – and – and –'

'And you're going to be sent away to strangers, and you're afraid,' said Mr Pink-Whistle at once. 'Here, take my hanky – it's bigger than yours and cleaner.'

The little girl rubbed her face with Pink-Whistle's hanky, and tried to stop crying. 'Yes,

I'm to go to somebody called Mrs Clamp, and she's got three boys all bigger than me, and a little girl who doesn't want me there. Mrs Clamp scolds people a lot, and I'm frightened.'

'What you want is somebody to love you, isn't it? said Mr Pink-Whistle. 'A real mother?'

'Oh, yes – wouldn't that be lovely!' said the little girl, beaming. 'You know – the kind of mother who welcomes you home from school and wants to know what you've been doing, and looks after you when you're not well, and makes you a cake on your birthday, and fills your stocking at Christmas, and says goodnight to you when you're in bed.'

'I know the kind of mother you mean,' said Mr Pink-Whistle. 'It's the kind of mother most children have. Dear, dear – what a pity that a nice little girl like you can't make some mother very happy.'

'I'd try my hardest,' said the little girl earnestly. 'But mothers all have children of their own and they don't want me. I suppose, Mr Pink-Whistle – I suppose you don't know any children who don't want their mother and would let me have her?'

'I know plenty of children who aren't good

or kind to their mothers,' said Mr Pink-Whistle, handing out another peppermint, 'but that doesn't really mean they want to give her away! This is a difficult problem, little girl. By the way, what is your name?'

'Alice,' said the little girl. She gave Pink-Whistle back his hanky. 'I'm all right now,' she said. 'It's nice to have you for a friend, Mr Pink-Whistle. I don't wonder that all the children love you.'

'Well, well – that's a nice thing to say,' said Pink-Whistle, pleased. 'Look here – I can't think what to do about you – but do you think your aunt would let you come and stay with Sooty – that's my cat – and me, for a day or two, whilst I look round? Has she heard of me?'

'Oh, yes,' said Alice. 'Sometimes she's read me stories about you, so she knows you already.'

Well, that's how it happened that Mr Pink-Whistle had little Alice to stay with him. Sooty was delighted. The little girl was so kind and willing. She wanted to do all kinds of jobs for Pink-Whistle, and you should just have seen how well she darned his socks, and mended a hole in his shirt!

She was sweet to Sooty, too, and helped her to clean the house, and even brushed the fur on top of her head, where Sooty couldn't reach to lick.

Mr Pink-Whistle couldn't seem to find anyone who would be a good mother to Alice. They all seemed so busy and worried and tired. It would never do to ask them to look after yet another child.

He talked to Sooty about it and Sooty had an idea.

'You know, Master,' she said, 'there's Miss Trot-About in the next village. She lives in Cherry Cottage, and –'

'Yes, I remember her,' said Pink-Whistle. 'Isn't she the one with five cats and a parrot?'

'Yes,' said Sooty. 'That's how I know so much about her. I know all the cats, you see. They say Miss Trot-About is the kindest, nicest person, who never forgets their fish and milk, and –'

'Yes, yes,' said Pink-Whistle, 'but if she's got all those cats to fuss about, surely she wouldn't want a little girl?'

'I think it's because she hasn't got a little girl or boy that she fusses over the cats,' said Sooty. 'She's the kind of person that's got to love somebody, you see, somebody of her own. Well those cats are hers, and she really does love them.'

'It's an idea,' said Pink-Whistle, thinking hard. 'Yes, it really is.'

He went over to see Miss Trot-About. She was feeding all her cats. He noticed that she was limping and walking with a stick.

'Good morning, Mr Pink-Whistle,' she said. 'Excuse my limping like this. I've got a very bad leg, and I really ought to be in bed for a bit – but there's nobody I can trust to see to my pussies.'

'Well!' said Mr Pink-Whistle at once, 'I wonder if you'd like a little friend of mine to come and see to them for you. She's staying with me now, and Sooty, my cat, loves her. She would be very pleased to come and look after both you and your cats, I'm sure. And the parrot, too.'

'Really?' said Miss Trot-About. 'Well, if she's a friend of *yours*, Mr Pink-Whistle, she must be all right. Bring her over. But mind – if I don't like her, back she comes the very next day!'

'Certainly, certainly,' said Pink-Whistle, and off he went, all the cats following him to the

gate. He whistled gaily as he caught the bus home. Had he managed to put a wrong thing right again? He would soon know.

He told Alice about poor Miss Trot-About and her bad leg, and all her cats and the parrot. Alice listened hard.

'She ought to be in bed for a little while,' she said. 'Mr Pink-Whistle, should I just pop over there for a day, and let her have a rest? I'm sure I could look after the cats – and the parrot, too.'

'Well, that certainly would be kind,' said

Pink-Whistle. And that's how it came about that Alice went over to stay with Miss Trot-About till her leg got better.

Miss Trot-About had only two bedrooms, her own and a little one under the eaves. It had a slanting roof, and a climbing rose looked in at the window. A small bed stood by the wall. Alice looked at the room in delight.

'Oh – am I going to sleep here?' she said. 'Oh, Miss Trot-About, I do love your house. It's a *home*, isn't it, not just a house. You've so many flowers about, and I like your bright cushions, and your clock has such a nice loud tick, and isn't it lovely the way the cats all curl up in their own baskets.'

'Dear me – what a long speech,' said Miss Trot-About, pleased. 'Now, do you think you can cook the fish for the cats, and give them their meal? And the parrot's cage wants cleaning out, and –'

'Oh, Miss Trot-About, of course I can do all that!' said Alice. 'I'd love to. But won't you get into bed and rest your leg? That's why I've come, you know – to look after things for you till your leg's better! The cats will be all right – see how they follow me about already!'

Well, Alice settled into that little cottage as

if she had lived there all her life. The cats loved her. The parrot talked to her all day long. Even the hens out in the garden came clucking when she called them.

Miss Trot-About stayed in bed for two days – then another day – and then another and another. She heard Alice trotting round, humming, talking to the parrot, fussing the cats, lighting the gas under the kettle, and generally sounding as happy as could be.

'I must get up tomorrow,' said Miss Trot-About each day. But she didn't. 'Oh, dear, I can't,' she said to herself. 'My leg is quite better. I'm a fraud, I know. But if I get up and show that I'm better, little Alice will go. I can't bear her to go. She's better than the cats, and a hundred times nicer than the parrot. If ever I'd had a little girl I would have wanted one just like Alice!'

Well, of course, Miss Trot-About had to get up at last! She got up really because Mr Pink-Whistle called to say he was coming to tea that day. That meant he would take Alice away. Alice watched her coming quite easily downstairs.

'Oh – your leg really and truly is better!' she said. 'I'm so glad!'

Oh, *dear*!' thought Miss Trot-About, 'she's glad I'm better so that she can go. I expect she's bored being here so long, poor child. Well, she really has been very good. I must give her a nice present.'

Miss Trot-About took hardly any notice of her cats! She didn't even speak to her parrot. She talked to Alice all the time, and fetched a little blue skirt she thought she could make into a dress for her, and asked her what her favourite cake was so that she could make it for tea.

Alice suddenly ran to her and gave her a hug. 'Do you know,' she said, 'you're *just* like a mother!'

Miss Trot-About was so surprised that she couldn't say a word. Well, well – that was about the very nicest thing anyone had ever said to her in her life. Just like a mother! Would you believe it?

Mr Pink-Whistle came to tea. He hadn't been near Alice and Miss Trot-About since he had left Alice at the cottage. He badly wanted to know what had happened. Did Miss Trot-About like Alice? Did Alice want to stay? Would they tell him some good news?

But they didn't. Miss Trot-About was sure

that Pink-Whistle had come to fetch Alice, and she was sure that Alice wanted to go.

And Alice was sure that Pink-Whistle was going to take her away, and perhaps send her to Mrs Clamp, and she was sure that Miss Trot-About wouldn't want her any longer now that she was better.

'Well – did you have a happy time together?' said Mr Pink-Whistle at last.

'Oh, very,' said Miss Trot-About. 'But I'm sure Alice is ready to go now.'

'A very, very happy time,' said Alice, 'but I'm sure Miss Trot-About will be glad to be on her own again.'

Mr Pink-Whistle sighed. What a pity! This was something he hadn't managed to put right after all.

'You'd better get your little bag,' he said to Alice. 'It's time we went. What a lovely tea that was, Miss Trot-About. Thank you very much.'

He went to help Alice with her bag. She was in her dear little room, tears in her eyes. 'I hate to say goodbye to it, Mr Pink-Whistle,' she said. 'It's so homely. And Miss Trot-About is just like a real mother. I do love her. I just hate to go. If only she would love me instead of her cats!'

'Now you just stay here a minute and dry your eyes,' said Pink-Whistle, taking her bag. 'Don't let Miss Trot-About see you crying. It would upset her.'

He went down with the bag and popped his head round the sitting-room door. 'Just going,' he said, and then he stopped in surprise. Miss Trot-About was dabbing her eyes with her hanky!

'Well – what's the matter with you?' said Pink-Whistle, quite expecting the parrot to burst into tears next.

'Nothing. Nothing, really,' said Miss Trot-

About. 'It's just that I shall miss Alice so dreadfully, and I'm such a fraud, Mr Pink-Whistle. My leg was better days ago, but I wouldn't get up because I wanted to keep Alice to the very last minute. I wish I was her mother. She's just exactly right for me. She's much better than five cats and a parrot. I do so wish she was mine!'

Alice came in just as Miss Trot-About said all this. She listened in the greatest surprise. Then she flew over to Miss Trot-About and put her arms round her.

'I heard you! Well, if you wish you were my mother, so do I! I won't leave you! Don't let me go, don't let Mr Pink-Whistle take me away!'

'I won't. He shan't,' said Miss Trot-About, suddenly looking so very fierce that Mr Pink-Whistle backed away in alarm.

'Go away, Mr Pink-Whistle,' said Miss Trot-About. 'I shan't allow you to take Alice away. This is her home. I won't allow you to send her to Mrs Clamp. What a very wicked thing to do!'

'And I won't leave Miss Trot-About,' said Alice. 'It's no good, Mr Pink-Whistle, I just won't come with you. I'm needed here. We love each other, and no matter *what* you say I'm going to live here with Miss Trot-About. So there!'

They both looked so fierce that Pink-Whistle hardly dared to say a word. He just said, 'Goodbye, bless you both,' and disappeared out of the door.

When he had gone, Miss Trot-About and Alice looked at one another. 'Do you know – I have a feeling that Mr Pink-Whistle meant this to happen?' said Miss Trot-About. 'He was just putting another wrong thing right. He didn't *want* to take you away. And instead of thanking him, we've been cross. Oh, dear!'

'Never mind. He'll understand,' said Alice. 'We'll ask him to tea again on Friday – and we'll have the most wonderful cake you ever saw, with "Thank you, Mr Pink-Whistle" on top of it. He's a darling.'

He is, of course – and I can just imagine how pleased he will be when he sees that cake, can't you?

Chapter 3

Mr Pink-Whistle Comes Along

'Sooty!' called Mr Pink-Whistle to his big black cat, 'I'm going out for a walk. It's a lovely, sunny winter's day. I'll be back in time for dinner.'

Sooty went to the door to see him off. He went briskly down the garden path and out of the gate. The frost crunched under his feet as he went, and the pale December sun shone down on him. What a lovely day!

'I think I'll go down to the pond and see if there are any children sliding on it,' he thought. So off he went, down the lane, up the hill, down the hill, and across a meadow where frost whitened the long grass in the ditches.

Mr Pink-Whistle was just putting his leg

over the stile to go to the pond when his sharp ears heard a sound. He had pointed brownie ears and could hear like a hare!

'Now, what's that?' he thought, a leg half over the stile. 'Is it an animal? Or a child? Or just a noise?'

It seemed to come from a little tumble-down shed by the hedge. Mr Pink-Whistle listened. Yes, there certainly was a noise – a sniffy sort of noise – sniff-sniff-gulp, sniff-sniff!

'I'd better go and find out,' said Pink-Whistle, and he got down from the stile and went to the little shed. He poked his head inside. It was rather dark and he couldn't see anything at first. Then he saw something white. 'Dear me!' said Pink-Whistle. 'Is that a face I see? Does it belong to someone? Who are you?'

The face was peeping out of a pile of hay in the corner. It spoke.

'Yes, but please go away. This is *my* shed. It's private.'

Pink-Whistle didn't go away. He was sure that he could see that the face was very miserable. He came right into the shed.

Somebody scrambled out of the hay,

crossly. It was a boy of about ten. 'I told you this was *my* shed,' he said. 'It's on my father's land and he said I could have it for my own. You're trespassing!'

'Was it you I heard sniff-sniff-sniffing?' asked Pink-Whistle. 'What's the matter?'

'Nothing,' said the boy. 'Nothing to do with you anyway. Don't you know when people want to be alone? I wish you'd get out of my shed.'

'I'm going,' said Pink-Whistle. 'But it's a pity you haven't even a dog to keep you company. If you're unhappy, it's nice to have a dog's nose on your knee.'

He walked to the door. 'Come back,' said the boy suddenly, in a shaky sort of voice. 'I like what you said just now. You might understand if I tell you something. You wouldn't have said that if you hadn't understood what friends dogs are, would you?'

'No,' said Pink-Whistle, turning back. 'So it's something to do with a dog, is it? Your own dog, I suppose.'

'Yes,' said the boy, sitting down on the hay and rubbing a very dirty hand over his face. 'You see, I've got no brothers or sisters, so my

dad gave me a dog for my own. My very own, you understand – not one that's shared by the whole family. Buddy was my own, every whisker of him, every hair.'

'That's a fine thing,' said Pink-Whistle. 'I expect that you belonged to him as much as he belonged to you. You were his friend as much as he was yours.'

'I'm glad you understand,' said the boy.

'It's nice to tell somebody. Well, Buddy's gone. Somebody's stolen him. He was a golden spaniel with big, loving eyes, and he cost my father a lot of money. That's why he's been stolen, because he's valuable.'

Sniff-sniff-sniff! The boy rubbed his hand over his eyes again. 'I'm ten,' he said, ashamed, 'and too old to make a fuss like this, like a four-year-old. I know all that, so you needn't tell me. But a dog sort of gets right into your heart if he's your own.'

'I shall begin to sniff, too, in a minute!' said Pink-Whistle. 'I know exactly what you feel. You're thinking how miserable your dog will be without you, and you're hoping that nobody is being cruel to him, and you're wondering if he's cowering down in some corner, puzzled and frightened. Well, that's enough to make anyone feel miserable.'

'He disappeared yesterday,' said the boy. 'Two men came to the farm to ask if they could buy chickens – and I'm sure they took Buddy away. They may have given him some meat with a sleeping-powder in it and got him like that. I don't know. The police say they can't trace the men and they haven't had any report of a golden spaniel anywhere.'

'I see,' said Pink-Whistle. 'Er – do you happen to know me by any chance, boy?'

'My name's Robin,' said the boy. 'No – I don't know you. I've never ever seen you before, have I?'

He peered closely at Pink-Whistle. The sun shone in at the little shed window just then and he suddenly saw Pink-Whistle clearly. He saw his green eyes and pointed ears, and he gave a little cry.

'Wait! Wait! Yes, I've seen your picture somewhere in a magazine or a book. Yes, I remember now. Why – surely you're not Mr Pink-Whistle?'

'I am,' said Pink-Whistle, beaming all over his face, pleased that the boy knew him. 'And I like to go about the world putting wrong things right.'

'Get back Buddy for me then, please, *please*!' said Robin, clutching hold of Mr Pink-Whistle's arm. 'I never thought you were real, but you are. Can you get back Buddy?'

'I'll do my best,' said Pink-Whistle. 'I'll go now. Cheer up, get out of this dark shed and go home and find some work to do. Perhaps I can put things right for you.'

He walked out of the shed. Robin ran after

him, suddenly very cheerful indeed. He was amazed. To think that Mr Pink-Whistle should have come along just then – what a wonderful thing!

Pink-Whistle went back home. He called Sooty, his cat, and told her about Robin. 'Go to the farm and speak to the farm cats,' he said. 'They will have noticed these two men and have seen if Buddy was taken away by them. Find out all you can.'

Sooty ran off, tail in the air. She soon came back with news. 'Yes, Master! The farm cats say that the men came back that evening, threw down meat for Buddy and then went away. Buddy ate it and fell asleep. Then the men came back and put him into a sack. They had a wagon drawn by a horse called Rip, who told the cats that his masters went to Ringdown Market every Thursday. You will find them there.'

'Thank you, Sooty,' said Pink-Whistle. 'That's all I want to know.'

The next day was Thursday. Pink-Whistle set off to Ringdown Market. It was a long way away, but he got there at last. What a babble of sound there was! Horses whinnying, sheep baaing, hens clucking, ducks quacking,

41

turkeys gobbling, geese hissing and cackling!

Pink-Whistle looked for a golden spaniel. There were three for sale at the market. Which was Robin's? Mr Pink-Whistle decided to make himself invisible. This was a gift he sometimes used, and he used it now!

One moment there was a kindly man walking about – the next moment he wasn't there at all! An old woman selling eggs was most astonished. She blinked her eyes in wonder and then forgot about it. Pink-Whistle went up to a golden spaniel. 'Buddy!' he whispered. 'Buddy!'

The dog took no notice. So that one wasn't Robin's dog. Pink-Whistle went up to the second spaniel and whispered. But he wasn't Robin's dog either.

'Buddy!' whispered Pink-Whistle to the third spaniel, who was lying miserably on some sacks behind two men selling hens. 'Buddy!'

The dog sprang up at once, his tail wagging. He looked all round. Who had called him by his name? One of the men turned round sharply.

'Lie down, you!' he said, and kicked him. Pink-Whistle felt very angry indeed. Ah!

These fellows wanted punishing. They wanted frightening. Well, he would have a fine game and give them a wonderful punishment.

He began to bark like a dog and Buddy pricked up his ears at once. Then Pink-Whistle pretended that Buddy was speaking.

'Hens, peck these men!' he cried. And then it seemed to the men as if a whole flock of invisible hens were all round them, pecking hard – but really, of course, it was Mr Pink-Whistle jabbing at them with his hard little forefinger – peck-peck-peck!

The men cowered back, squealing. Everyone came to see what the matter was. Pink-Whistle began to cluck and that made the men think there really were invisible hens pecking them.

Then Pink-Whistle called out again in a barking sort of voice, so that it seemed as if Buddy was talking: 'Geese, attack these men!'

And dear me, what a cackling there was from old Pink-Whistle then, what a hissing – and what a jab-jab-jabbing from top to bottom of the scared men. Everyone stared, amazed. *What* was happening? Where did the cackling and hissing come from? Who was jabbing at the men?

'Serves them right,' said somebody. 'I never did like those two.'

And then, oh dear, Pink-Whistle decided to be a butting goat! What fun he was having – and what a wonderful punishment he was giving the two men!

'Goat, butt them!' he cried, and the men looked everywhere, scared, wondering if an invisible goat was coming at them.

Biff! Pink-Whistle ran first at one man and then at another. Biff! Bang! Biff! The men felt exactly as though a big, rather solid goat was butting them back and front. Pink-Whistle butted one man right over and he rolled on top of Buddy. Buddy promptly snapped at him and growled.

Pink-Whistle immediately growled too, and talked in his growling. 'Bull, toss these men!'

The men gave a loud howl. Hens had pecked them, geese had jabbed them, a goat had butted them! Surely, surely they were not going to be tossed by a bull, and an invisible one, too, coming at them from any side!

'Run for it!' yelled one man, and he ran for his life. The other followed. Pink-Whistle galloped after them, making his feet sound like a bull's hooves – clippitty-clippitty-clop. How the men howled!

Pink-Whistle couldn't follow them very far because he laughed so much. How he laughed! People were really very puzzled to hear loud chuckles and not to see any one there.

'Well, I don't know what's upset those two fellows,' said a burly farmer, 'but I'm glad to see the back of them. Rascals, both of them!'

Pink-Whistle went back to where the dog Buddy lay on the sacks, puzzled and frightened. Buddy suddenly heard a quiet, kindly voice talking to him, and invisible fingers undid the knot of rope that tied him to a rail.

'Come with me, Buddy,' said the voice, and Buddy went obediently. He sniffed at Mr Pink-Whistle's invisible legs. How very peculiar to smell legs that didn't seem to be there! Buddy couldn't understand it – but then, he didn't really understand anything that had happened since he had left Robin. His world seemed quite upside-down and not at all a nice place.

It was a long way to the farm where Robin lived – but as they got nearer to it Buddy became very excited indeed. His nose twitched. He pulled against the hand on his collar.

'Not so fast, Buddy,' said Mr Pink-Whistle. 'I want to come with you.'

Buddy took another sniff at the invisible legs. Well, they smelt all right, so the person with them ought to be all right, too. He trotted along obediently, getting more and more excited.

It was dark when at last they came to the farm. Buddy was now so excited that he pulled and pulled at Pink-Whistle's hand.

The little man led him to his kennel. 'Get in there and wait,' he ordered. 'And bark. Bark loudly!'

Buddy crept in and then he barked. How loudly he barked. 'Wuff-wuff-wuff, WUFF-WUFF. Robin, I'm back, where are you? WUFF-WUFF!'

And Robin heard, of course. He would know Buddy's bark anywhere! He sprang up at once, his face shining. 'Mother! That's Buddy's bark! He's back!' he cried, and raced out of the house to the yard. He came to the kennel, calling joyfully.

'Buddy! BUDDY! I'm here!'

And, before Buddy could squeeze past the invisible Mr Pink-Whistle, there was Robin, squeezing into the kennel! He got right in, and then you really couldn't tell which was boy and which was dog, they hugged and licked and rolled and patted, and yelped and shouted so joyfully together!

At last, tired out, they sat peacefully together in the kennel. Buddy's nose on Robin's knee and Robin's arm round Buddy's neck. Only Buddy's tongue was busy, lick-lick-licking at Robin's hand.

'Buddy! I do wish I could say a big thank you to Mr Pink-Whistle!' said Robin. 'I don't even know where he lives, though. I'd say, Mr Pink-Whistle, I'm your friend for ever and ever!'

Pink-Whistle heard it all. He was peering in at the kennel, as happy as could be. He had put a lot of wrong things right in his life, but surely this was one of the very best! He stole away in the darkness, a very happy little man indeed.

Chapter 4

Mr Pink-Whistle's Little Trick

One winter's afternoon, just as it was getting dark, Mr Pink-Whistle walked down a road near a school.

'Let me see – it's just about the time that the children come out of afternoon school,' said Mr Pink-Whistle, trying to see the time by his watch. 'I'll watch them as they go by. Perhaps one or two of them will know me!'

So he stood by a shop and waited. Soon he heard chattering and clattering – and out came all the children from the school down the road.

Two small girls came first, talking together. They walked along and didn't notice Pink-Whistle. Just as they had passed him, another child ran up – a big boy. As he passed the two

little girls he swerved and bumped into them both.

Down went one of them – and the other was sent into the nearby wall. They screamed.

The boy roared with laughter and ran on. 'It's Sam again!' said one girl, picking herself up. 'Horrid thing – why does he always have to bump into people when he passes them? I suppose he thinks it's funny.'

'Your coat is all muddy,' said the other little girl. 'Your mother will be awfully cross! How I hate Sam! He's always so rough.'

Mr Pink-Whistle was just going to go up to the two children to see if he could do anything about the little girl's coat when they ran off together. He frowned. What a horrible boy! Did he really make a habit of bumping into others like that?

A small boy came by with his satchel on his back – and suddenly someone swooped down on him, bumped into him and knocked him flying!

'You beast, Sam!' yelled the small boy. 'Lying in wait for me again! I'll tell my father.'

'Pooh!' shouted back Sam, and shot off across the road. Mr Pink-Whistle went to help the small boy to pick up his books. They were lying in a puddle.

'Oh – thanks,' said the boy. 'Gosh, I shall get into a row – all my books soaked! Blow Sam! I bet he's hiding somewhere near to bump into as many of us as he can. He's so big, you see – the biggest of our class.'

It was rather dark now and the little boy couldn't see Pink-Whistle clearly. How pleased he would have been if he had known who it was that was helping him!

A girl came along after that, and two more behind her. Pink-Whistle stood nearby, watching out for the horrid Sam. Was he hiding somewhere again so that he could rush out at these children, too?

Yes – he was! Whoosh! He shot across the road and bumped heavily into the first little girl – and then swung round to bump into the others. Pink-Whistle shouted a warning to them.

'Hey – look out!'

They just got out of Sam's way in time and he almost crashed into the wall himself. He peered into the shadows angrily, trying to see who it was that had warned the two girls. He was afraid that it might be a policeman, and he shot off into the darkness.

Pink-Whistle felt sure that he wouldn't appear again, and he set off down the street, wondering if he could do anything about this tiresome Sam.

Suddenly someone came running behind him, and bumped hard into him, giving him a shove at the same time. A shout of laughter told Mr Pink-Whistle that it was Sam again!

Over went the little man like a skittle – Sam was certainly good at bumping! Pink-Whistle found himself sitting in a big patch of soft mud – most unpleasant!

'Ha! Sam again, I suppose!' he said, angrily. 'I'm small – so he thought I was a child. Well, it's certainly time he was stopped – and I'll soon stop him, too!'

Pink-Whistle got up, caught a bus and went home to his little cottage. He told Sooty, his cat, all that had happened. Sooty grinned. She put Pink-Whistle's coat to dry, and made him some tea.

'You want to get the old Wobbly-Man to walk down the street,' she said. 'It would give Sam a most unpleasant surprise to find someone he couldn't possibly push over!'

'Good idea,' said Pink-Whistle. 'And what about me walking down the pavement carrying a nice bunch of prickly holly, Sooty?'

'I'd like to be there and see Sam bumping into that!' said Sooty. 'And what about putting a hat and a pair of boots and a coat on a great big balloon, and putting a walking spell into the boots?'

Pink-Whistle nearly fell off his chair with laughing. 'Oh dear – you do think of peculiar things,' he said to Sooty. 'Yes, we'll certainly do the balloon idea. You see, it's just too dark to see properly at that time in the afternoon – so Sam won't be able to see who he's bumping, and as I and the Wobbly-Man are both small, he will think we are children and become rushing full speed at us!'

'And he's sure to want to bump into someone who looks nice and fat like the Walking Balloon,' said Sooty. 'Well, you're certainly going to have some fun tomorrow, Master!'

Pink-Whistle went to see the Wobbly-Man after he had had his tea. The Wobbly-Man nodded and smiled. He was always ready for a

joke. He had no feet at all, only a curved base, and he got along by wobbling himself fast. Ha! He would give Sam a shock tomorrow!

'Nobody's ever knocked me over yet,' he said to Pink-Whistle, 'and nobody ever will! I'll be along tomorrow, Pinkie!'

The next morning Pink-Whistle gathered some fine holly out of his garden – two big armfuls. Then he sent Sooty to buy a balloon, a long one, not a round one.

He blew it up as big as ever he could, but he had to put a bit of magic into his blow because he wanted a rather big balloon. He stuck an old top-hat on it with glue and put a pair of old boots at the bottom, also stuck on with glue – very strong glue it was, too!

He slipped a walking spell inside each of the boots, and then draped an old brown coat round it – it really did look most peculiar!

Sooty began to laugh. 'I *must* come and watch!' she said. 'I really must! Please let me, Master!'

'Well, I shall want you to pick up the boots, coat and hat when Sam bumps into Mr Balloon and bursts him, pop!' said Mr Pink-

Whistle. 'So you can come. First I'll walk along with the holly – then I'll tell the Wobbly-Man to do his bit – and then we'll set Mr Balloon walking along on his magic boots!'

At four o'clock the next afternoon the Wobbly-Man, Mr Pink-Whistle, Mr Balloon and Sooty were all waiting for Sam. The children came out from school in a bunch that afternoon, because that was the only way they could stop Sam from bumping into them. He was too much of a coward to tackle a lot of children together.

Sam was cross. Blow! Wouldn't some child run home alone? Well, he would hide and see. So, as usual, he slipped into a doorway and watched.

The children ran down the street – and then, when there was nobody there, Sooty whispered to Pink-Whistle.

'Now's the time to begin, Master – I can see Sam watching from that doorway.'

Mr Pink-Whistle slipped out of his hiding-place and began to walk down the dark street. Sam saw him – and thought he was a child, because Pink-Whistle was small. He raced out of the doorway and ran behind Pink-Whistle.

Just as he was about to bump him, Pink-Whistle swung round with his armful of holly!

'Ooooooh! Ow!' yelled Sam, finding his face and hands pricked with the sharp holly. 'What is it? Oooh, I'm hurt!'

He stopped to nurse his hands and feel his face. Whatever had that child been carrying? Then he saw the Wobbly-Man coming along. At least, he could just make out someone waddling towards him – who was it? Ah, perhaps it was old Fatty, who was in the form above him! Sam grinned.

He rushed at the Wobbly-Man and gave him an enormous bump. The Wobbly-Man wobbled over sideways and then wobbled back so violently that he gave Sam a sharp knock that nearly sent him flying! Sam was most surprised – and very angry.

'Don't you dare to fight *me*!' he said. 'I'll shove you right over, see?' And he gave the Wobbly-Man another tremendous push that made him wobble to and fro very fast indeed.

Sam watched him, a sturdy wobbling shadow in the dark street. Why didn't *Fatty* fall over? He pushed hard again, but all he could do was to make the Wobbly-Man wobble faster and faster.

'You're not Fatty!' cried Sam, suddenly frightened. 'You're not! Who are you? I don't like you. Stop wobbling, do stop wobbling. I won't push you again, I promise.'

But, of course, the Wobbly-Man had to wobble, no matter where he went, and Sam watched him wobble away into the darkness, wondering whatever he was.

'Funny!' said Sam to himself. 'Very, very funny. Most peculiar. Anyone would think that that fellow couldn't walk, the way he wobbles as he goes. I don't like it. I'll just give someone else a good shove, and I'll go home.'

So he waited. The next person that came down the dark street was a tall man. Sam didn't dare to run and bump into him – no, tall men had a habit of reaching out and giving him a jolly good shake!

Ah – here was someone coming – someone short, with a silly top hat on his head. Sam grinned. Whoever it was that was coming was walking very near the holly hedge – it would be fun to push him right into it. Let someone else feel what it was like to be pricked all over! Sam's hands were still sore with the scratches they had had.

Of course, it was Mr Balloon this time! Pink-Whistle had set the spell going in the boots, and the long-shaped balloon, dressed in old top hat, old coat and boots was now walking down the street.

'It's just a silly old tramp,' said Sam, catching sight of him in the light of a lamp. 'I'll give him such a shock – one of my very BEST BUMPS!'

So he ran from the doorway where he stood and bumped into the Balloon-Man. He shoved him hard against the holly hedge – and all the prickles ran into the balloon. BANG!

San nearly jumped out of his skin. He stared at where the old tramp had just stood – but he had completely disappeared! Sam couldn't see the top hat, boots and coat lying in a little heap half-under the hedge.

'Ooooh! He's gone! He went BANG and disappeared!' howled Sam. 'What have I done? What's happened! Help! Help!'

The Wobbly-Man, who had wobbled back on the other side of the road, and had joined up with Pink-Whistle again, laughed till he cried. Pink-Whistle laughed too, and Sooty ran to collect the hat, boots and coat.

Other children heard Sam's calls for help and ran up to him. 'What's the matter? What's up?'

'I bumped into somebody and got pricked all over, look!' said Sam, and he was actually crying! 'And then I bumped into somebody else, and he wobbled over and wobbled back and hit me – he was horrid! And then I bumped into a silly old tramp with a top hat

– and he went BANG and disappeared. I'm frightened!'

'Serves you right,' said a small boy. 'Now all you want is someone to bump into you and you probably wouldn't *ever* shove people about again!'

The children went off together, grinning. They didn't feel in the least sorry for Sam – it would teach him a lesson!

Sam went down the street too, sniffling miserably. He didn't mean to bump into anyone else he met that evening! What with pricks and wobbles and bangs, he had had quite enough.

Someone padded behind him. Someone soft bumped violently into him! Over went Sam and rolled into the same patch of mud into which he had bumped so many others. He sat up and yelled.

'Sooty!' said Pink-Whistle's voice. 'Sooty – you shouldn't have bumped into him like that – you really shouldn't. Look how muddy he is!'

'I couldn't help it!' said Sooty. 'Really, Master, but he'll *never* bump anyone again!'

Sooty's right – and do you know, when the children heard all about Sam's strange

61

adventures the next day, one boy looked very wise, and said:

'It rather sounds as if old Mr Pink-Whistle was around last night, Sam. You'd better be careful!'

Now, however did he guess?

Chapter 5

Mr Pink-Whistle Gets a Letter

One day a letter popped through Mr Pink-Whistle's letter-box.

Sooty the cat picked it up and took it to her master.

'A letter for you, Master – marked URGENT,' said Sooty.

'Ah,' said Pink-Whistle. 'It looks as if it is from a child – so it certainly *is* urgent.'

He opened the letter and read it out aloud to Sooty:

'Dear Mr Pink-Whistle,

'I do hope this gets to you. I'm a little girl called Katy, and I live with my mother. We haven't much money, but we have a nice lot of hens, and they lay eggs, which we sell.

'But somebody comes and takes the eggs. We

63

don't know who it is, but it is very serious for us because we do need the money we get for the eggs. We hardly have any to take to market now.

'You go about the world putting wrong things right, dear Mr Pink-Whistle. Do you think you can put *this* right?

Your loving friend,

KATY.'

'P.S. – I know about you because of the stories I've read.'

'What a nice little girl she sounds!' said Sooty. 'Will you help her, Master?'

'Of course!' said Pink-Whistle. 'I'll go along this very day. Look up a bus to – let me see, what's the address – Tipkin-on-the-Hill. I've never been there before.'

Sooty went off to get the bus timetable, and soon Mr Pink-Whistle had discovered the bus that went to Tipkin-on-the-Hill. He put on his hat, said goodbye to Sooty, and set off. Nobody took much notice of the funny little man on the bus, except two children who noticed his pointed ears and green eyes.

'He's like Mr Pink-Whistle!' whispered one to the other. 'Oh – suppose he *is*!'

Mr Pink-Whistle didn't say a word, he just twinkled at them. Then he suddenly made himself invisible – and the two girls stared at his empty seat in surprise. They didn't know that he had got up very quietly, tiptoed to them, and slipped big bars of chocolate into their school-bags! How exactly like Mr Pink-Whistle to do a thing like that.

When he got to Tipkin-on-the-Hill he went

to find Katy. She was feeding the hens, and they were clucking round her – cluck-cluck-luck-luck-cluck! Cluck-cluck-luck-luck-cluck! Then the cock stood up straight and crowed. He had suddenly seen Mr Pink-Whistle, and he knew him.

'Cock-a-doodle-doo! We're pleased to welcome YOU! Cock-a-doodle-doo!'

'Good morning, Katy,' said Mr Pink-Whistle, and the little girl swung round at once. She stared in delight.

'Oh! You've come! Oh, you really are Mr Pink-Whistle, aren't you?' said Katy.

'Yes, I really am,' he said. 'I'm sorry to hear of your trouble. Tell me about it.'

Katy told him. 'Somebody comes and takes the eggs at night – and often in the daytime, too! Our cottage is lonely, as you see – and when I'm at school and Mummy is at work, anyone can slip in here and steal the eggs.'

'I'll find out who it is,' said Pink-Whistle. 'Don't you worry any more. Are your hens laying well?'

'Not very,' said Katy. 'So we can't spare the ones that are stolen! Oh, Mr Pink-Whistle, fancy *really* seeing you! I never, never thought you really *would* come!'

66

'I can't *always* come when people are in trouble,' said Pink-Whistle. 'But I happened to have nothing to do today. Now – isn't it time you were off to school?'

'Yes, it is,' said Katy. 'I shan't tell anyone at school about you, Mr Pink-Whistle, or they'll all be out here to see you – and you'd never be able to find out who the thief is. But I don't know *how* I'm going to keep such a wonderful secret!'

She ran off to school and left Mr Pink-Whistle in the hen-run. He turned to the hens and the big, beautiful cock. 'Cluck-luck-luck!' he said, speaking the language of the chickens. 'It's my belief you know the thief. Cock-a-doodle-doo, tell me who – who – who!'

The chickens all talked back at once, clucking and cackling loudly. Mr Pink-Whistle nodded. 'Thank you, I'll give him such a fright!'

The little man went into the hen-house and shut the door. He made himself quite invisible, sat down in the corner and waited. Nobody was about at all. Katy's mother was still out at work, and Katy was at school.

The hens clucked and cackled together in

the run outside. Then suddenly the cock crowed loudly, and Mr Pink-Whistle listened.

'Cock-a-doodle-doo, a visitor for *you*!' Then the door of the hen-house opened and someone crept in. It was quite a shock to Mr Pink-Whistle to see the thief so well-dressed – he had expected someone down-at-heel and ragged.

'So this is Mr James Pinch, the thief,' thought Pink-Whistle, watching the smart-looking young man as he went to the nesting-boxes one after another and took the eggs there. He slipped them into his big pockets, and then crept out again. Pink-Whistle followed silently.

Mr Pinch went to a big house and in at the kitchen entrance. Pink-Whistle followed.

The man came to a woman in a big white apron, who was bending over a great stove.

'Here you are, Cookie,' said the young man, and he handed her out the two dozen eggs or so that he had in his pockets. 'That's one pound fifty, please. All new-laid! I bought them in the market.'

Dear, dear – what a story-teller! Pink-Whistle shook his head and made up his mind that this young man wanted a shock.

And Pink-Whistle would give him one – oh, yes, a very peculiar shock that would teach him a lesson, too!

Mr James Pinch went off to his room to change into his uniform. He was a footman and waited at the table of Lord and Lady High-Up. Pink-Whistle went with him, and sat on his bed, quite invisible, while he changed his clothes.

'Cluck-luck-luck!' said Pink-Whistle, sounding exactly like a hen. 'Cackle-cackle-*squawk*!'

The young man was extremely startled. He jumped and looked round. 'Cackle, cackle, cackle,' said Pink-Whistle, exactly as if he had laid an egg and was proud of it.

Mr Pinch felt really most alarmed. He looked under the bed for any hidden hen. He looked behind the chest.

'Cock-a-doodle-DOOOOO!' said Pink-Whistle, just behind him. The young man almost jumped out of his skin.

'What is it? Where's that hen – and now a cock!' he said, angrily, feeling very scared. 'There's nothing here – not even a feather.'

'CLUCK!' said Pink-Whistle in his ear, and the young man rushed out of his room in a fright. He tore down the stairs and into the kitchen. The cook was there, and the maids, and the butler, all talking together.

'What's up, Jamie?' said the cook, as the young man rushed in, panting. Before he could answer, Pink-Whistle began clucking again. 'Cluck-cluck-cluck-cluck-CLUCK! Cluck-cluck-cluck-cluck-CLUCK!'

'A hen! A hen in my kitchen!' said the cook, and took up a broom to chase it out. 'Where did it come from? We have no hens here!'

But she couldn't find it, of course, Pink-Whistle sat on a chair and chuckled to himself. Then he began again.

'Cackle, cackle, cackle – CACK! Cack-cack-cack-CACKLE!'

'There now – it must have laid an egg!' cried one of the maids. 'But where is it? Is it in the larder?'

The larder door was opened, and Pink-Whistle slipped inside, bending down under the shelf, still quite invisible.

'Cock-a-doodle-DOO!' he crowed as loudly as he could.

'Well, if there isn't a cock about now, too,' said the butler. 'I never heard of such a thing! Where *are* the creatures?'

'Look here – we'd best not waste any more time in looking,' said the cook. 'My dinner will be late, and then My Lady High-Up will have plenty to say!'

Pink-Whistle took a rest. He waited till the footman went into the dining-room at dinner-time, to wait on Lord and Lady High-Up. Then he went, too, still invisible. He stood just behind Jamie Pinch.

'CLUCK!' he said, right in Jamie's ear. 'Cackle CACKLE! Sqqquawk!'

Jamie jumped and dropped the dish he was holding. CRASH! The butler frowned, and so did My Lady. Jamie picked up the bits and ran from the room. Pink-Whistle ran behind him. 'Cock-a-doodle-DOO!' he crowed in delight. Poor Jamie nearly fell over in fright. He looked round for the cock but there wasn't one there. He took another dish from the cook and hurried back. Pink-Whistle hurried after him.

'Cluck-cluck-cluck!' said Pink-Whistle, just behind Jamie, as he came into the room. The butler swung round angrily. 'Jamie! What are you thinking of? Stop doing that!'

'But – but – but,' said Jamie, just exactly at the same moment as Pink-Whistle said, 'Cluck-cluck-cluck!' So it sounded as if Jamie were clucking!

'Get out of this room,' said Lord High-Up. 'Any more of this nonsense and you'll lose your job.'

'Cock-a-doodle-DOO!' crowed Pink-Whistle at the top of his voice, and Jamie rushed out of the room. Pink-Whistle went, too, following him very closely.

'Here comes Jamie again!' said the cook. 'What's up with him? And bless us all –

there's that cackling noise again! Where's it coming from? Jamie, do *you* know anything about it?'

'No, I don't!' said Jamie, looking very scared at the loud, cackling noise just near him. 'Everywhere I go, I hear it.'

'It must be something to do with *you*, then,' said the cook. 'We didn't hear it when you were in the dining-room. Sometimes it's a hen, sometimes it's a cock!'

Pink-Whistle obligingly became both. 'Cluck-cluck, cock-a-doodle, cackle-cackle, doo!' he said, clucking and crowing loudly. Jamie gave a scream and ran into the scullery.

'Cock-a-cluck-a-cackle-doodle-doo!'   he heard just behind him, and sat down with his head in his hands. What a dreadful evening – but it hadn't ended yet. Pink-Whistle clucked and clacked, cackled and crowed – and once he forgot himself and did some very lifelike quacks as well! Jamie thought he must be going mad. He went up to his bedroom and lay down.

Some feathers were coming out of a hole in his pillow. Pink-Whistle smiled to himself and pulled out a handful. Then he sat down on the floor and pretended to be a hen and a

cock fighting. He scrabbled on the floor –
and then suddenly flung the feathers up into
the air.

Jamie watched in alarm. Now these awful
creatures were fighting – tearing feathers out
of each other. He groaned and shut his eyes.
'I'll *never* go near a hen again!' he said.

Pink-Whistle spoke in his own voice then –
a very solemn, deep and stern voice. 'Who
steals eggs? WHO steals eggs? And then he
gave the answer, crowing like a cock. 'Cock-a-
doodle-doo! It's you, you, YOU!'

'Oh, who is it?' said Jamie in alarm. 'Tell
me, tell me! I'm sorry, very sorry, and I'll
never do it again. I'll give Katy all my savings
to make up for what I've done.'

'Do, do, DO!' said Pink-Whistle, pleased. 'Do, DO!'

Jamie got up and took a money-box from a cupboard. He slipped out of his room and down the stairs. He ran all the way to Katy's, with Pink-Whistle close beside him.

Katy was just shutting up the hens, looking sad because eggs had been stolen again that afternoon. Jamie rushed up to her and put the money-box into her hands.

'Katy! I stole your eggs – I've stolen them for a long time, even though I knew you and your mother were poor. Please forgive me. I'll never do it again. See, I have brought you all my money.'

Katy was too astonished to say a word. She took the box, and Jamie at once ran off again. How glad he was not to hear any more clucking or cackling or crowing in his ear that night. What a fright he had had!

Mr Pink-Whistle!' said Katy, in a low voice. 'I know it's all because of you! Mr Pink-Whistle, are you here? I want to thank you.'

'Dear me, I forgot I was invisible,' said Mr Pink-Whistle, and immediately said the words that made him visible once more. Katy saw the dear little fellow standing there, beaming at her, and ran to him.

'Take half the money!' she said. 'Oh, how clever you are! What did you do?'

'The money is all yours and your mother's,' said Pink-Whistle. He told Katy what a fright he had given to Jamie, and the little girl laughed till she cried. 'Oh, I wish I could have heard you!' she said. 'I do wish I could!'

'It was very funny,' said Pink-Whistle. 'I really enjoyed it. I'm glad you wrote to me, Katy dear – I do like to put wrong things right, as you know.'

He kissed her goodbye and went, humming a little song.

'Cock-a-doodle-doo,
I've lots of things to do,
When things go wrong
I come along
And see what I can do.
Yes, I see what I can do,
Cock-a-doodle-doo!'

I really do like Mr Pink-Whistle, don't you?

Chapter 6

Well Done, Mr Pink-Whistle

One afternoon, when Mr Pink-Whistle was enjoying a little nap in his garden, his cat Sooty came up to him.

'Please, Master, wake up,' she said. 'There's a little girl come to see you, and she says it's important.'

Pink-Whistle woke up with a jump. 'A little girl – important?' he said, blinking at Sooty. 'Bring her here at once. Little girls are always important to me – and little boys, too!'

So Sooty brought a little girl of about nine years old to Pink-Whistle. She gazed at him shyly. 'I hope I haven't disturbed you, Mr Pink-Whistle,' she said. 'But I managed to get your address from a little boy you once helped.'

'And what have you come to see me for?' asked Mr Pink-Whistle. 'Sooty, bring some lemonade and your new buns.'

Sooty ran off and came back with a tray of home-made lemonade and chocolate buns. 'What a lot of buns for only two people,' said the little girl.

'But surely you can eat five or six new-made chocolate buns!' said Mr Pink-Whistle. 'Help yourself and tell me what you've come for.'

'Well, it's about a boy called Peter,' said the little girl, taking a bun. '*Peters* are usually nice, but this one isn't. In fact, he's really horrid, and you see, nobody can do anything about him. So I thought perhaps you could.'

'Well, you know, I don't like people to tell tales,' said Pink-Whistle. 'Are you sure you ought to tell me about this Peter? And tell me your name, too please, I'd like to know.'

'I'm Geraldine,' said the little girl. 'Oh, aren't these buns nice! Did Sooty really make them? You know, Mr Pink-Whistle, I've read all about you in a book; that's how I know that you go about the world trying to put wrong things right. And I think that's a lovely thing to do.'

Pink-Whistle liked this little girl. He was sure she hadn't come just to tell tales. He poured her out some more lemonade.

'I'll tell you about Peter,' said Geraldine. 'It isn't really telling tales. The other children all asked me to come to you for help.'

'Well, tell away,' said Pink-Whistle, 'and do have another bun. Eating always helps talking if you've got something to say, and I can see you have.'

'Oh, do you think that, too?' said Geraldine. '*I* always think so. Well – Peter is a big boy at our school, and he hasn't got a bicycle. Most of us have, but he hasn't.'

'Go on,' said Pink-Whistle.

'So he borrows ours,' said Geraldine. 'He never *asks* us if he can – he just takes them. He rides nearly all the way to his home on them, then jumps off, throws them into a hedge and walks the rest of the way home.'

'I see. And whoever owns the bicycle he has taken has to catch the bus home,' said Pink-Whistle.

'Well, no – because usually we haven't the bus-money if we ride bicycles,' said Geraldine. 'So we have to walk home and we're late and get scolded. We get scolded about our bikes, too. But nobody can stop Peter. We don't like to tell tales of him to the teacher, or to our mothers – you see, Mr Pink-Whistle, he's very big and strong.'

'I see,' said Mr Pink-Whistle again. 'Do have another bun. Sooty will think you don't like them if you leave any. I suppose this Peter does quite a lot of other things besides taking people's bicycles.'

'Oh, yes,' said Geraldine. 'But I needn't bother you with those. You can guess them.'

'I think I can,' said Pink-Whistle. 'Pulling hair – slapping – pushing and pinching – all the things a big boy does when he's a bit of a

80

bully. But I suppose what you want my help for is about this bicycle business.'

'Yes, please,' said Geraldine. 'Last week Jimmy was given a lovely new bike for his birthday and promised to keep it clean – and two days ago, Peter borrowed it, and left it out in the rain all night in a hedge. Now Jimmy's father has taken his bike away for a month because it looks dreadful!'

'Well, I think I can cure Peter,' said Pink-Whistle. 'Tell me the address of your school, please. And do have another bun. Don't waste them!'

'I've *never* tasted such lovely buns,' said Geraldine. 'But I'm not going to take the last one, thank you very much.'

She said goodbye and shook hands. Pink-Whistle took her to the gate, thinking how nice it was to meet children with good manners. You just couldn't *help* liking them!

Next morning Pink-Whistle made himself invisible, as he often did, and went along to find Geraldine's school. Ah – there it was – and there was the bicycle shed. Pink-Whistle looked at the bicycles – what a lot! Plenty for that bad boy Peter to choose from!

Pink-Whistle went down the row of bicycles

81

rubbing each back wheel and muttering
something. Ah, he knew plenty of useful
spells! He stood up straight and smiled. Now
Peter, look out! If you take a bicycle today,
you'll be sorry!

Well, Peter did, of course. He was out
before any of the other children and ran to
the shed. He picked out Benny's because it
was nice and shiny. He was out of the school
gate before anyone could stop him, riding at
top speed!

He went down this road, and that, on his
way home – and then suddenly he looked
astonished. He ought to be in Hacking Road
– but he wasn't. He was in a road he didn't

know at all. How could he have taken a wrong turning? He turned round and rode back to the corner. There was a signpost there that Peter didn't remember at all. He stared at it in surprise. It pointed four ways.

One way said '*To Mr Whack.*' Another said '*To Hard Work Village.*' A third said '*To The Dragon*' and the fourth said '*To The Crosspatch Witch.*'

Peter couldn't understand it. He had never in his life seen the signpost before. He didn't want to go to any of the people or places it pointed to. Good gracious! What was he to do? Had he lost his way?

He couldn't stay by the signpost all day so he got on his bicycle again and rode off in the direction of *Mr Whack.* He didn't like Hard Work – he didn't want to meet a Dragon – and he certainly didn't like the sound of the Crosspatch Witch! He didn't much like Mr Whack's name, either!

He was not at all pleased with Mr Whack when he found him! He rode down the lane, round a corner, and came to a small house. He jumped off, meaning to ask his way home.

He knocked at the door – and out came a big man with a whippy little cane!

'Ha!' he said, 'I'm Mr Whack, and I'm glad you've come to see me. I've heard about you. You take bicycles, don't you? Hold out your hand!'

Peter didn't want to, but his hand held itself out – and then the other hand held itself out, too. Whack, whack, whack – how that whippy little cane enjoyed itself! But Peter didn't. Like all bullies, he was a coward, and he howled loudly.

'There – that's what happens to bullies,' said Mr Whack. 'Leave the bicycle. I'll see that it's returned to its owner. Go over that stile, and you'll see the way home.'

Peter went off, still howling. He climbed over the stile, and went across the field. When he came to the other side he found, to his great astonishment, that he was in the lane that led to his home. He simply couldn't understand it.

He didn't take anyone's bicycle the next day. His hands smarted too much to hold bicycle handles! But the day after he took Geraldine's! He raced out of the school gates on it, laughing to think of the little girl's anger and dismay when she found it was gone.

And will you believe it, the bicycle took him to the same signpost as before! There it stood, its four fingers pointing to *Mr Whack, Hard Work Village, The Dragon*, and *The Crosspatch Witch*. Peter stared in horror.

How had he come here again? He couldn't imagine! Well, he wasn't going to Mr Whack this time, that was certain. But he didn't want to go to Hard Work Village either – or to the Dragon or the Witch.

He decided to take the road that led to the Dragon. 'It can't possibly be a *real* dragon,' said Peter to himself. 'There aren't any dragons now. It must be a hotel called the "Dragon". I'll ask there for my way home.'

But, you know, it *was* a real dragon! As Peter rode on round the corner, he saw a gate right across the road, and beside it was a cave. He got off his bicycle to open the gate – and suddenly out of the cave came a dragon.

He looked very like the one that St George fought long ago, but he had remarkably kind eyes.

'Wait!' he called, in a roaring voice. 'Are you good or bad?'

'What do you mean?' said Peter. 'And who

are you? I don't believe in dragons. You're just somebody dressed up!'

'I'm not,' said the dragon. 'Ah – now I know you. You're Peter, the boy who takes bicycles, aren't you?'

Peter began to feel as if he was in a bad dream. 'No, I don't take bicycles,' he said quickly. 'Let me go through this gate, please, whoever you are.'

'I can't,' said the dragon. 'Not until I've fought you.'

'What do you mean! I don't fight dragons!' said Peter, scared.

'Well, you see, I'm a good dragon,' said the dragon, 'so I fight bad things and bad people. *Bad* dragons fight good people. You're bad, so I must fight you. Look out for yourself!'

And the dragon ran at poor Peter, who turned and fled for his life! The dragon sat down and laughed. He was rather disappointed too. He really was a very good and kind creature, and hadn't had a fight for years, but sometimes he felt he *would* like to hit out at something bad.

Peter fled down the road and came to a little wood. He saw a path there and raced down it, afraid that the dragon might be

following him. And quite suddenly he came
to a part he knew – how strange! Why, just
down there and round to the left and he
would come to a road he knew quite well!
How had he managed to get to that strange
signpost again?

Peter was very, very puzzled when he got
home. What a horrid adventure! Why did the
bicycles keep taking him to that signpost
instead of to his home? Was there a spell on
him? He didn't believe in spells, but certainly
something peculiar was about.

He remembered that little Geraldine had
said she was going to ask Mr Pink-Whistle for
help. Well, he didn't believe in any Pink-

Whistles either. But suppose – just suppose Geraldine *had* gone to him, wasn't this just the kind of thing that Pink-Whistle would do?

Peter went out into the garden to think. Should he ask Geraldine if she had found Mr Pink-Whistle? No, she wouldn't tell him anyway.

'Oh, I wish I knew what was happening to me!' groaned Peter. 'Why do those bicycles take me the way I don't want to go? I believe it's all something to do with Mr Pink-Whistle. I'd tell him a few things if he were here!'

'Well – I *am* here,' said a quiet voice, and suddenly, in front of Peter, Mr Pink-Whistle appeared bit by bit – first his head, then his hands and legs, then his body. It was really very strange. Peter didn't like it at all.

'Now tell me whatever you want to,' said Pink-Whistle. 'I'll listen.'

'No, I don't want to say anything,' said Peter.

'Not even about bicycles?' said Mr Pink-Whistle. 'I wonder whose bicycle you will take tomorrow, Peter – and where you will go? You're having some adventures, aren't you? You must enjoy taking those bicycles from the other children!'

'I don't! I don't! And I won't any more, either!' cried Peter. 'I won't go to those horrible places, so it's no use your putting spells on the bicycles. I'll never touch one again! Never!'

'Peter! Who in the world are you talking to?' called his mother, coming into the garden. At once Mr Pink-Whistle disappeared, and was quite invisible. Peter gave a gulp and ran indoors up to his bedroom.

Well, as you can guess, Peter never took anyone's bicycle again – and will you believe it, when his father offered him one of his own for his birthday, he said no!

'What! You've been pestering me for a bicycle for *three* years – and now I can buy you one, you say no!' said his father. 'You don't mean it, surely?'

But Peter *did* mean it, and you can guess why he didn't want one. He was afraid it would take him to that peculiar signpost again!

Chapter 7

Mr Pink-Whistle and the Scribbler

One day, when Mr Pink-Whistle was sitting in his garden, he saw the front gate open, though he could see nobody there.

'Now, what –' he began, in surprise – and then he saw a tabby cat slip through the gateway, shut the gate behind him, and run to the back door.

'Ah – a friend of Sooty's, I suppose,' thought Mr Pink-Whistle, and turned back to his book. Before he had read two pages, Sooty, his cat, came walking out to him, and behind him came the tabby cat, looking rather shy.

'Mr Pink-Whistle,' said Sooty, 'this is a friend of mine – Paddy-Paws. He is a very good and honest cat – but he is most upset because somebody has been scribbling lies about him on a wall.'

'Dear me!' said Pink-Whistle, in surprise. 'Well, Paddy-Paws, I wouldn't take any notice of that.'

'It isn't so much himself he has come about as his little mistress, Fanny,' said Sooty. 'This boy who scribbles on walls writes horrible things about Fanny, too, and they make her cry. Paddy-Paws says she's sweet and kind, and he's most upset about it. He wants to know if you can help him.'

'Yes, Mr Pink-Whistle,' said the tabby, finding his tongue suddenly. 'You do put wrong things right, don't you?'

'I try to,' said Pink-Whistle, 'But what is it you want me to do, Paddy-Paws?'

'Well, sir, stop this boy from scribbling more horrible things,' said the tabby cat. 'I'll take you to the wall he scribbles on and you'll see the dreadful things he writes. Everybody can read them, sir, and they get very upset. But this boy is big and strong, and nobody can stop him.'

'Well, I'll come along now,' said Pink-Whistle, and he shut his book, 'Lead the way, Paddy-Paws!'

So Paddy-Paws led the way. Over a field, across a stile, down a lane, through a small village, along a high road and into another village. Pink-Whistle padded along with him. Sooty had been left behind at home.

Paddy-Paws came to a wall – and there, written in different coloured chalks, were a great many horrible sentences. Pink-Whistle read them out loud. ' "Betty is a cry baby. Katie is a tell-tale. George is a cowardy-

92

custard."' Pink-Whistle began to frown. 'Dear, dear – what things to write for everyone to see! Most unpleasant!'

He went on reading. '"Fanny is a thief. She took my rubber at school. Paddy-Paws is a thief, too. He steals fish from the fish shop."'

'I never did steal fish, you know,' said Paddy-Paws, pulling at Pink-Whistle's trousers. 'And my little mistress, Fanny, isn't a thief. She's honest and truthful and good. And Betty isn't a cry baby – but she can't help feeling miserable when her tooth aches, can she? And George isn't a coward, and –'

Pink-Whistle frowned as he looked at the rows of nasty writing on the wall, and read on further – '"Old Mrs Brown is mean. Nancy cheats at sums." Good gracious me, what an unpleasant person this boy must be!' said the little man. 'What's his name, Paddy-Paws?'

'Harold, sir,' said the tabby cat. 'Look – here he comes, with one of his bits of chalk!'

In a trice Pink-Whistle made himself invisible. Paddy-Paws stared round and about in surprise. Where had this nice little man gone to so suddenly?

'I'm still here, but you can't see me,' said Pink-Whistle, in a whisper. 'You go home now, Paddy-Paws, and leave this boy to me. I'll soon cure him.'

Pink-Whistle went up close to Harold's back, and watched what he was writing. Harold wrote very clearly and quickly. 'Ellen took some apples off Mr Henry's tree when he wasn't there.'

Just as he was finishing this, a boy and girl came up. 'Hello, Ellen!' said Harold, with a big grin. '*I* saw you up that apple tree. You're a bad girl!'

Ellen gave a scream when she saw what Harold had written. 'You horrid boy! Mr Henry *said* I could pick six apples because I fed his hens for him. And oh, look, George, he has written that you're a coward. Fight him!'

But George, the boy with her, was very small, much smaller than the big Harold. He stared at Harold, and tried to speak boldly. 'You're NOT to write things like this, you're –'

But he didn't say any more, because Harold knocked him right over, bang, wallop! Ellen pulled George up to his feet and they both ran away at once. Harold was too big to fight!

When Harold left the wall and walked away,

whistling, Mr Pink-Whistle followed him, still invisible.

He was quite surprised at all the things that Harold did on his way home.

He slipped into Mr Henry's field and took three pears growing on the wall there. He went into old Mrs Brown's garden and cut her washing-line so that all the clean clothes fell to the ground. He chased a small kitten up a tree and then threw stones at it.

Pink-Whistle was amazed. To think that a bad boy like this dared to write horrible things about other children, where everyone could read them! He followed Harold very closely indeed. What was this awful boy going to do next?

Harold walked by the greengrocer's shop. Outside were boxes of all kinds of goods. Harold took a quick look round to make sure no one was about and quickly picked up two bananas. He put them under his coat. Pink-Whistle could hardly believe his eyes!

Then Harold saw a small boy walking down the road and ran quietly behind him. He snatched the boy's cap off his head and threw it over a garden hedge up into a tree. The boy swung round fiercely, but when he saw

Harold, he said nothing. Harold was so big and strong!

Pink-Whistle watched everything that Harold did. He followed him all the way home and indoors. He saw him tiptoe to the larder and take two jam tarts. He saw him take some chocolates out of his mother's box. What a dreadful boy!

Soon Harold's mother came home from her shopping. 'Hello, dear,' she said, 'have you had a nice day at school?'

'Yes,' said Harold. 'I was top in class. The other children are so stupid. Katie's a tell-tale, and Fanny is a dreadful thief, and George is an awful coward.'

'Your father will be pleased to hear you were top again,' said his mother. 'Here he comes. Put the kettle on for tea, Harold.'

Pink-Whistle stood quietly in a corner behind the couch, out of the way of the family as they got tea and sat down to it. Then the little man crept out of his corner, still invisible, and put his hand into the right-hand pocket of Harold's coat. He pulled out some pieces of coloured chalk. Ah – Pink-Whistle was going to have a fine time now!

'Fanny is an awful thief,' said Harold,

eating his bread and jam. 'She stole my rubber yesterday and today she took my best pencil.'

Just as he finished, there came a faint squeaking sound from the big bare wall opposite the table. It was made by the red chalk that Pink-Whistle was suddenly using to write with!

Everyone stared in amazement as a line of very neat writing began to appear on the wall. The words followed one another fast.

'Harold is a thief. He stole two bananas from the greengrocer's shop. He stole three

pears from Mr Henry's wall-trees. They are in his pockets now.'

Harold's father stared at the writing in the greatest astonishment. 'What's all this?' he said. 'Who's written that? Have you *really* stolen pears and bananas, Harold?'

There came another line of writing.

'Harold is a coward. He knocks down children smaller than himself. He is cruel. He chased a tiny kitten up a tree. He is unkind. He threw a small boy's cap over a garden hedge.'

Harold sat glued to his chair, his eyes following the strange writing that went on and on across the wall. He began to whimper, because he was so frightened.

'Harold is a cry baby,' wrote the chalk. 'Look at him whimpering now! He took two jam tarts from the larder. He stole two chocolates from the box over there. He –'

Harold gave a loud cry and rushed over to the wall, pulling his hanky out of his pocket as he ran. He rubbed it over the wall, so that it smudged and blurred the writing.

But Pink-Whistle immediately went to the next wall and went on writing there!

'Harold cut Mrs Brown's washing-line

and made all the clothes fall to the ground. He –'

'Oh! Harold – surely that wasn't *you* who did that!' said his mother. 'Mrs Brown told me someone had cut her line – oh, Harold, what is all this writing? Who is doing it?'

'It is Mr Pink-Whistle,' wrote Pink-Whistle. 'I have seen the wicked things that Harold scribbles on walls, so I am doing the same to him. But the things I write are true, and what *he* writes is untrue!'

'*Mr Pink-Whistle!*' said Harold, in fear. He had read many tales of the little half-brownie man, and he knew all about him. He snatched the chalk as it wrote, and felt round and about for Pink-Whistle – but he was safely behind the couch again, still quite invisible!

Pink-Whistle gave a little laugh. 'Beware, Harold!' he said. 'Whenever you write on walls outside, I shall come and write on your walls here. If *you* can do it, so can I!'

And with that he skipped over the couch, went to the window and jumped neatly out. He set off home, longing for a cup of tea. Sooty was most interested to hear all that had happened!

'Now, Sooty, I want you to go each night

and see if anything is written by Harold on that wall,' said Pink-Whistle, drinking a nice hot cup of tea. Sooty nodded. She went that very night, with Paddy-Paws – but, dear me, someone had been along and wiped the wall clean!

'That's Harold!' said Paddy-Paws. 'I saw him go by with a duster. I guess he won't ever scribble on walls again, Sooty!'

For a whole week Sooty went to look at that wall, but it was as clean as could be. Harold wasn't going to have Pink-Whistle coming along to his home and writing things about *him*! That wasn't funny at all.

Paddy-Paws was very grateful. He caught three rats in Pink-Whistle's garden and laid them in a row on his front doorstep to show him how grateful he was. Pink-Whistle was surprised to see them there!

'Thank you, Paddy-Paws,' he said. 'I'm always pleased to put wrong things right, you know. Tell me, if you want my help for anyone, another time!'

He's nice, isn't he? I'd love to have a friend like old Pink-Whistle!

Chapter 8

Mr Pink-Whistle's Cat is Busy

One day, just as Mr Pink-Whistle was about to go and catch the train to visit his old aunt, Sooty, his cat, came running to him.

'Master – there's a black cat with white paws come to see you. He wants your help.'

'Well, Sooty, I can't miss my train,' said Pink-Whistle. 'See if you can help him. After all, you're a cat too, and you know my ways – you can surely put right whatever the cat has come about. You can use anything out of my spell-cupboard if you like.'

'Thank you, Master,' said Sooty, and waved goodbye to Pink-Whistle from the door. Then she shut it and went to the back door where the black cat with white paws was waiting patiently.

'*I* will put things right for you,' said Sooty, rather grandly. 'What's the trouble, Whiskers?'

'Well, it's the man next door,' said Whiskers. 'He's a thief, Sooty, and a very sly one. He only takes small things, usually what he can put into his pockets, or carry in his hands. I've known about him for years, of course, but I've never bothered about him till today.'

'Why today?' asked Sooty, taking the cat indoors. 'Help yourself to the milk in my saucer – it's nice and fresh. Now tell me everything!'

'Well, I belong to a very kind old lady,' said Whiskers. 'But she's going a bit blind, and she can't see as well as she used to – and this man next door – Mr Gubbs his name is – keeps coming in, pretending to ask how she is – and each time he pops something into his pockets – perhaps a sausage roll from the larder, or a book from the bookshelf, or even something from my old lady's purse.'

'How wicked!' said Sooty. 'Just because the old lady can't see!'

'Yes. And this morning my old lady missed the stick she uses when she goes for a walk,' said Whiskers. 'It's a fine black one made of ebony, with a shining silver handle, and she's very proud of it. Now it's gone.'

'Did this Mr Gubbs take it?' asked Sooty.

'Of course he did! He came in to see the old lady this morning, and patted her hand, and asked her how she was – and told her not to come and see him out of the door, he knew the way all right – and he took the stick out of the hall-stand. He thought nobody saw him – but *I* saw him! I was sitting in a dark corner of the hall, watching.'

'It's a pity you aren't a dog,' said Sooty. 'Then you could bark at him and bite him.'

'I've tried hissing loudly, and putting out my claws if he comes near me,' said Whiskers.

'But he kicks me, and I'm afraid of him. Wouldn't Mr Pink-Whistle help? He likes to put wrong things right, doesn't he?'

'He's gone away. *I* can help instead,' said Sooty. She went to Mr Pink-Whistle's cupboard and looked at all the strange bottles and boxes there. She suddenly caught sight of a small bottle with blue-green liquid inside, and she laughed. She took it down.

'Look,' she said, 'this is a funny spell – it makes any tongue talk, and –'

'But that's silly – tongues always do talk,' said Whiskers.

'Not *all* tongues!' said Sooty. 'Not the tongues of shoes, for instance! Look, Whiskers, if you can manage to rub this spell on the tongues of Mr Gubbs' shoes, they will soon chatter away and tell the world about him – and *he* won't know who's doing the talking!'

Whiskers laughed so much that he fell into the saucer of milk. 'Give me the bottle,' he said. 'I'll manage to spread the spell on the tongues *somehow*. Oh, what a time I'm going to have!'

He hardly waited to say goodbye to Sooty, but ran off with the bottle in his mouth. And that night, when Mr Gubbs was in bed, and his shoes were in the kitchen, waiting to be cleaned, Whiskers hopped in at the kitchen window and ran over to them. He poured a little of the blue-green liquid over the tongues of the shoes, and then rubbed it in.

'Now talk, shoes, talk as much as you like when Mr Gubbs wears you,' he mewed. 'Tell the world about him and what he does!'

Well, next morning, Mr Gubbs put on his shoes as usual, and wondered where he could go that day to pick up a few more things that didn't belong to him. Yes – he would go round the market. It was market-day, and there would be plenty of chances for him to take this or that.

So off he went. On the way he met Mr Jaunty and managed to take his nice, blue silk handkerchief out of his pocket as he passed by. Then, when he passed Miss Jinky's house, he saw a lovely pink rose blossoming by the wall, and he snipped it off and put it in his buttonhole.

At the market he wandered round, smiling at people he knew, nodding politely, and stopping to say a few words to this person and that. He also managed to pocket half a pound

of butter when Mrs Plump, who owned the butter stall, wasn't looking, and to put a handful of ripe cherries into his pocket.

Then little Nicky and his sister came by and he offered them each a cherry from the ones in his pocket. 'Oh, thank you!' said Nicky. 'Are they out of your garden?'

'Yes, I picked –' began Mr Gubbs, but another voice interrupted him. 'He took them from the cherry stall,' said the voice. 'Oh, he's clever, he is!'

'Pooh – call that clever?' said another voice. 'I call it cunning – sly and cunning!'

Mr Gubbs was extremely startled. He looked all round for the talkers, but there was no one near except the two children, and *they* were looking most astonished. They gave him back the cherries at once and ran off.

'Now look here – who said that?' began Mr Gubbs and heard a peculiar husky laugh

somewhere near. It came from the tongue of
his right shoe, but he didn't guess that, of
course.

He went on his way, feeling puzzled and
soon met Mr Burly, the farmer.

'Hello, Gubbs!' said the farmer. 'Do you
want to buy fresh farm butter? Go to my stall
and –'

'He doesn't want any,' said a small voice,
loudly. 'He's got some in his pocket – it's a bit
squashy.'

'He took it from Mrs Plump's stall when
she wasn't looking,' said another voice. 'Oh,
he's an artful one! He wants watching!'

'Er – good morning,' said Mr Gubbs to the
astonished farmer and hurried off, his face
flaming red. *Who* was it talking about him like
this? He looked behind him. Was it some
irritating children who had been following
him? No – there was nobody near.

Old Lady Smiles came bustling up. 'Oh,
good morning, Gubbs. My word, that's a
beautiful rose you have in your buttonhole.
What's its name?'

'Er – I think it's called Beauty,' said Mr
Gubbs. 'I – er – picked it from my garden
this –'

'He picked it off Miss Jinky's best rose-bush when he passed by her garden this morning,' said a little voice, quite clearly. 'Nobody was looking.'

'You can't believe a word he says!' said the second voice. 'Not a single word. Horrible old Gubby!'

The other shoe-tongue gave its husky little laugh. 'What about the blue silk hanky? I saw him take it out of Mr Jaunty's pocket. Did you?'

'Oh, yes! I've just as good a view as you have of all his goings-on,' said the other shoe-tongue. 'I remember when –'

'Good morning to you, Gubbs,' said Lady Smiles, stiffly. 'I don't know if you can hear what I can hear – but I must say that I think it's all very extraordinary. *Good* morning!'

It soon got round that there was something peculiar about Mr Gubbs that morning, and to his great distress one person after another came up – just when he didn't want them! He must, he really *must* find out about those voices! As for the shoe-tongues, they had a perfectly marvellous time!

'Look – there's Mrs Grocer coming – she doesn't guess that old Gubby took a tin of

biscuits from her shop last week! Hoo-hoo-hoo!'

'And here comes old Mr Woosh. What would he say if he knew that Gubby took his tin of tobacco and popped it into his pocket, when he went calling on him the other day?' said the other tongue. 'It's no good his asking for it back either – it's all gone up in smoke!'

'Hoo-hoo-hoo!' laughed the other voice. 'You are very funny this morning. Ooooh, I say, look – here comes the policeman – and Gubby doesn't like the look of him!'

Indeed Gubby didn't! He was now so scared of what the extraordinary voices were saying that all he wanted to do was to run back home, shut his door and hide. But the policeman had been very, very interested in some of the things that the market-folk had told him about Mr Gubbs, and he wanted to make a few enquiries.

Gubby began to walk away quickly, and the voices shouted loudly, 'He's scared! He knows he's got that butter in his pocket!'

'And his socks belong to Mrs Jinky's husband – he took them off the line the other night!'

'And he took the vest he's wearing, too! And what about his watch? Wouldn't the policeman like to know about that! Hoo-hoo-hoo!'

Mr Gubbs took to his heels and ran, panting hard, hoping that the policeman hadn't heard a word. If only he could leave those voices behind! They must be somewhere in the market, nasty, mysterious voices. Once he got home he wouldn't hear them any more.

But he did, of course! As soon as he was indoors and the door shut, he sat down, out-of-breath – and the first voice began again.

'He can run fast, can't he? My word, I got quite giddy, going up and down, didn't you?'

'Yes, I did. We shall have some more fun soon, though – the policeman will be along, and a few others. Old Gubby's going to get what he deserves at last, the mean old fellow. I never did like him, did you?'

'Why – it's my *shoes*!' shouted Gubby, and he took them off and ran out into the backyard. He took off the dustbin lid and threw in the shoes. Then back he went and put on his slippers. They had no tongues, thank goodness!

But, it's no good, Gubby. There's a tramping down the street, and soon there will be a knocking at your door! You'll have to answer some very awkward questions, and when your house is searched you will find yourself marched off to the police-station. So shiver in your slippers, Gubby – the time has nearly come. Ah – rat-a-tat-TAT!

Sooty, Mr Pink-Whistle's cat, was longing to know all that had happened, and she was very glad to see Whiskers coming along the next day, looking as if he were bursting with news.

'Sit down. Tell me everything!' said Sooty, and Whiskers began. He told the whole story – he related everything that the shoe-tongues had said, and he told how Gubby had at last been found out and taken to prison.

'How do you know all this?' asked Sooty,

wiping tears of laughter from her eyes. 'Did you follow Gubby to market?'

'No. But, you see, he threw the shoes into the dustbin and I heard them talking to each other there, and went to rescue them. I took them out of the dustbin and they told me everything that had happened – every word they had said, and I laughed till my whiskers nearly fell off!'

'Where are they now?' said Sooty.

'Oh, they thought Mr Pink-Whistle might like to lend them to someone else some day,' said Whiskers. 'So they walked here with me. They're outside the door. Thanks very much, Sooty, for helping to put a wrong right all by yourself. My mistress has got back her ebony stick and she is very happy.'

And off went Whiskers, grinning, very pleased with himself. 'goodbye,' said a shoe-tongue as he passed the shoes. 'You certainly did us a good turn when you rubbed that blue-green polish into us – we've never had such a fine time in our lives. Thank goodness we don't belong to Mr Gubbs any more.'

'Nasty old Gubby! Hoo-hoo-hoo!' said the other tongue.